Dear Parents,

Welcome to the Scholastic Reader series. We have taken over 80 years of experience with teachers, parents, and children and put it into a program that is designed to match your child's interests and skills.

Level 1—Short sentences and stories made up of words kids can sound out using their phonics skills and words that are important to remember.

Level 2—Longer sentences and stories with words kids need to know and new "big" words that they will want to know.

Level 3—From sentences to paragraphs to longer stories, these books have large "chunks" of texts and are made up of a rich vocabulary.

Level 4—First chapter books with more words and fewer pictures.

It is important that children learn to read well enough to succeed in school and beyond. Here are ideas for reading this book with your child:

- Look at the book together. Encourage your child to read the title and make a prediction about the story.
- Read the book together. Encourage your child to sound out words when appropriate. When your child struggles, you can help by providing the word.
- Encourage your child to retell the story. This is a great way to check for comprehension.
- Have your child take the fluency test on the last page to check progress.

Scholastic Readers are designed to support your child's efforts to learn how to read at every age and every stage. Enjoy helping your child learn to read and love to read.

—**Francie Alexander**
Chief Education Officer
Scholastic Education

For James, Jordan, Julia, and Will
—G.M.

For Grace Maccarone and Edie Weinberg,
my two great teammates.
—B.L.

Library of Congress Cataloging-in-Publication Data is available.

ISBN 0-439-20139-X

10 9 8 7 6 5 4 3 2 1 03 04 05 06 07

Printed in the U.S.A. 23
First printing, April 2001

Softball Practice

by Grace Maccarone
Illustrated by Betsy Lewin

Scholastic Reader — Level 1

SCHOLASTIC INC.
New York Toronto London Auckland Sydney
Mexico City New Delhi Hong Kong Buenos Aires

Softball practice
is at four.
Sam gets his stuff,
runs out the door.

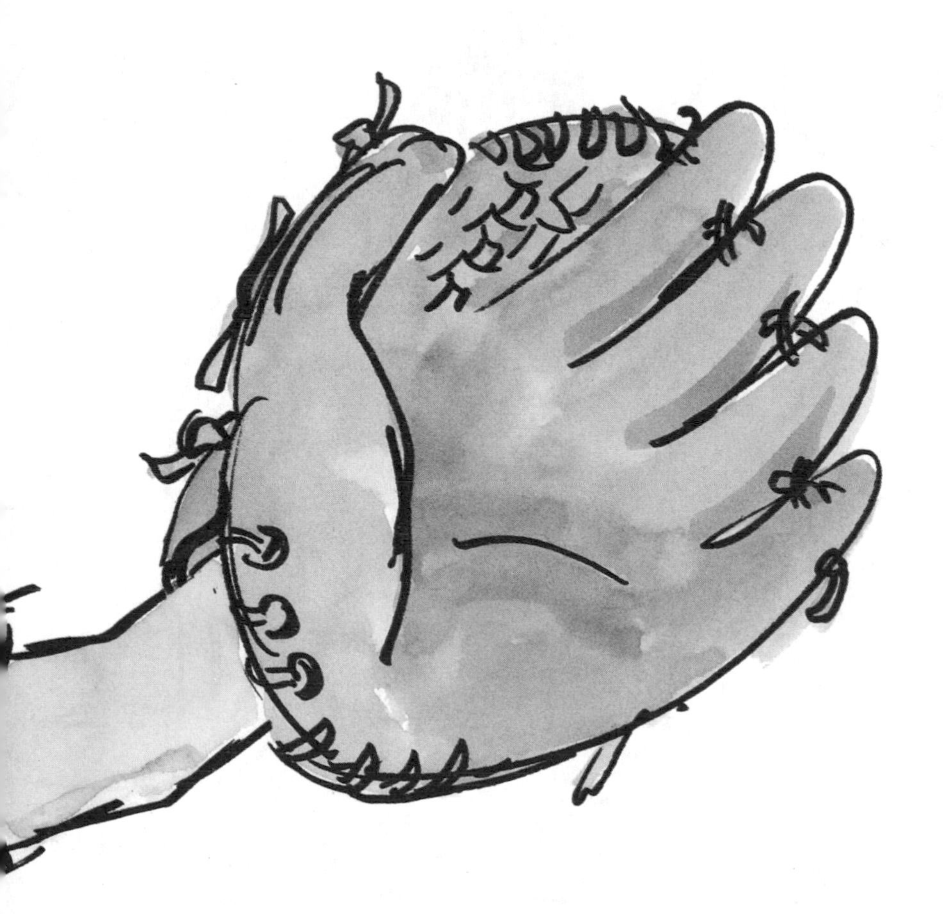

He goes inside
a yellow van

and says hello
to his friend Jan.

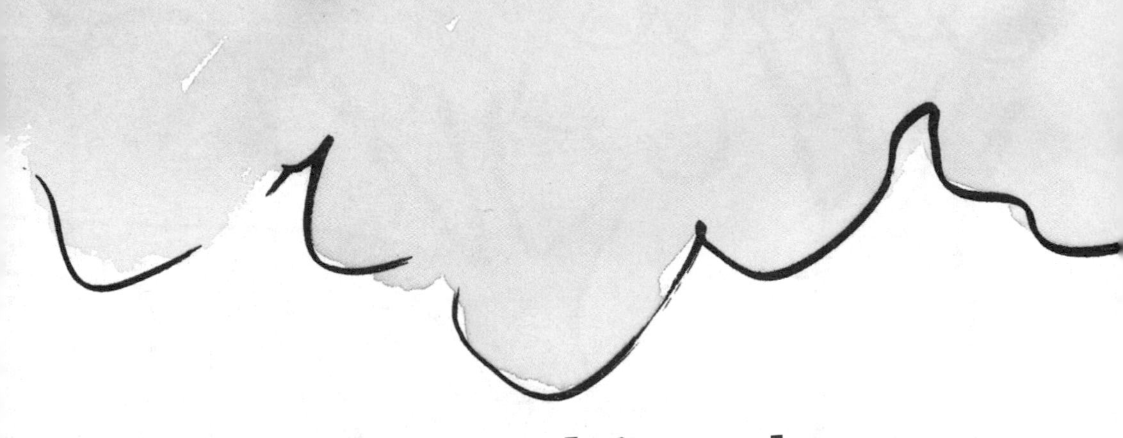

Aunt Gracie drives them
to a park . . .

but doesn't stay.
She drives away.

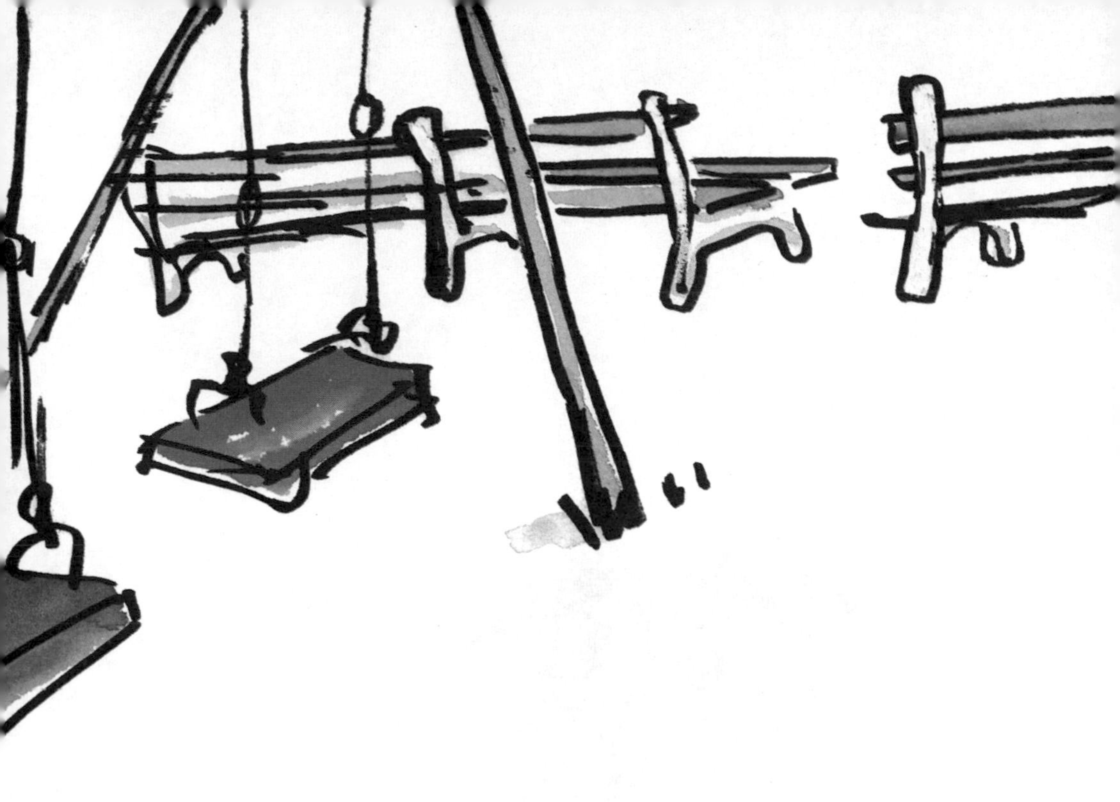

“We’re first,” says Sam.
“We have to wait.”
And so they wait . . .

and wait . . .

and wait.

And then Sam says,
"It's getting late.
We are waiting too long.
Something is wrong."

A worried look
is on Jan's face.
She says, "My Aunt Grace
left us at the wrong place."

Sam says,
"Don't worry, Jan."
Sam says,
"I have a plan.

“You throw to me.
Then I’ll throw to you.
We will practice together.”
And that’s what they do.

Jan is up. Sam pitches.

Jan swings.

And they run.
They practice together.
They have lots of fun.

Now here comes Sam's mom.

And here comes Jan's dad.

And here comes Aunt Gracie,
feeling quite bad.

There are hugs for all.

Then everyone plays ball!